SECOND STAR
to the left

Written by Jackie Andrews
Based on an original story by Graham Ralph

Illustrated by Paul Shardlow

First published in 2001 by BBC Worldwide Limited
Woodlands, 80 Wood Lane, London W12 0TT

ISBN 0 563 53326 9

Based on the original animation *Second Star to the Left*, produced by
Silver Fox Films and Link Entertainment for the BBC.
Licensed by Link Licensing.
From an original story by Graham Ralph.

Printed and bound in Belgium by Proost NV

Christmas Eve, and the stars were twinkling over a snow-covered countryside where children had built a jolly snowman. Now the children were asleep, dreaming of Santa Claus in his sleigh, bringing them their Christmas presents.

This is the story of just one of those presents, meant for a little girl called Polly…

"One thousand three hundred and one… one thousand three hundred and two…"

Archie, the rabbit, was gazing out of the window of the garden shed he shared with his guinea-pig friend, Duke, and was counting the stars. There wasn't much else to do.

"There must be more to life than sitting in our cages all day," sighed Archie. "A world of adventure is just waiting out there…!"

Duke was lying back in his cage, contentedly munching mince pies.

"Personally, Archie, I rather like it here," he said between mouthfuls. "Room service… central heating… and the bedding gets changed every day." He gave a loud burp.

Suddenly, high up in the sky – too far for Archie to see – a sleigh pulled by six reindeer swooshed past overhead in a flurry of hooves and stardust. It was driven by a jolly, bearded gentleman wearing a red suit, roaring with laughter.

"Ho, ho! Christmas Eve!" he laughed. "How I love it!"

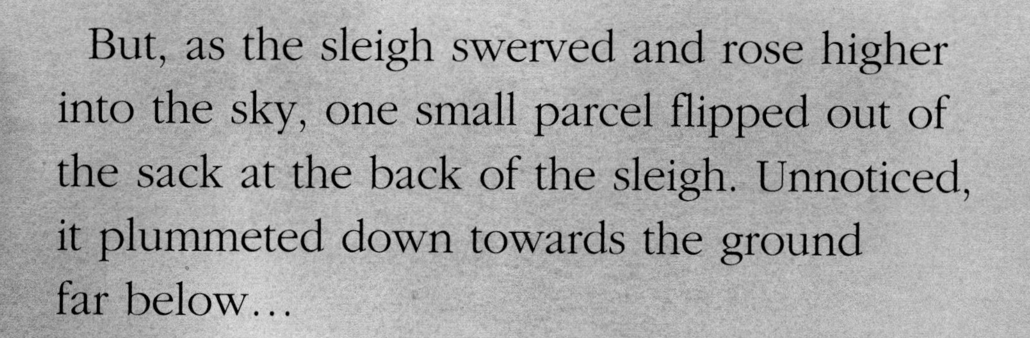

But, as the sleigh swerved and rose higher into the sky, one small parcel flipped out of the sack at the back of the sleigh. Unnoticed, it plummeted down towards the ground far below…

With an almighty CRASH, the parcel burst through the roof of the shed and landed among some bags of hay, just missing Archie.

Archie and Duke gazed at it in silent astonishment.

"What happened? Are we dead?" asked Duke.

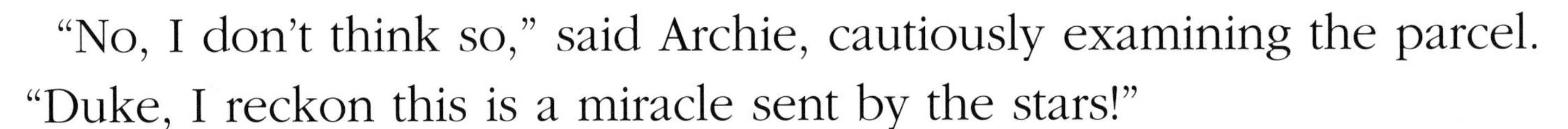

"No, I don't think so," said Archie, cautiously examining the parcel. "Duke, I reckon this is a miracle sent by the stars!"

"Yeah, right," said Duke. "But what does it do?"

"Er… I'm not exactly sure," said Archie. "But we'll ask Babs. She's bound to know."

When they reached the house, Archie had to toss a few snowballs up at Babs' window before he caught the hamster's attention. She'd been jogging in her exercise wheel.

Babs knew exactly what the parcel was as soon as she saw it.

"It's a Christmas present," she told them. "Humans give them to each other at this time of year. And I reckon someone's gonna be really sorry in the morning when this doesn't show up!"

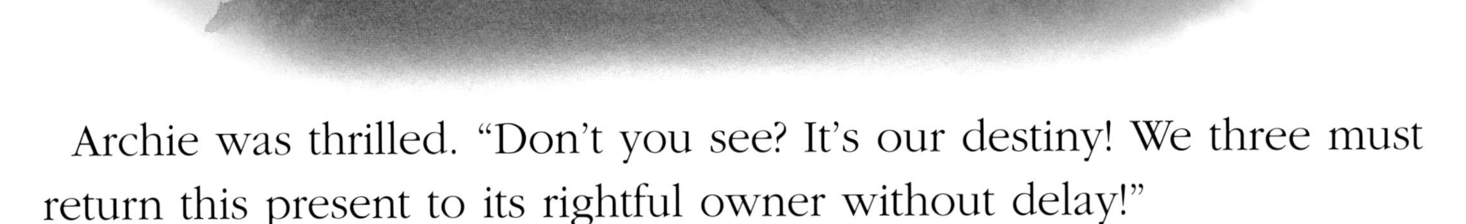

Archie was thrilled. "Don't you see? It's our destiny! We three must return this present to its rightful owner without delay!"

But Duke was doubtful. He didn't want to give up his home comforts.

"Hang on, what's this?" said Babs. She had found a label on the box. "Erm... 'To dear freckle-faced... um... Polly... love Santa.'"

Duke didn't want to know. He backed away.

Then Babs gripped Duke's whiskers.

"If we don't get this present to Polly by morning, Duke, she'll be broken-hearted. Is that what you want?"

Duke gulped. "I suppose I could do with some exercise," he said, weakly.

They heaved the present onto an old skateboard and pushed it out of the shed. As luck would have it, the snowman in the garden was able to tell them where to find Polly – but not before Archie had poked him with a twig and demanded his co-operation.

"Polly helped to build me," said the snowman. "She lives down in the village at the bottom of the hill. Just follow the second star to the left!"

Gingerly, they set off down the hill with the parcel on the skateboard. Babs perched on the top with Archie and Duke at each end.

"Steady, boys," urged Babs. "Not too fast now!"

Unfortunately, the slope was much too steep and slippery. Before long, the skateboard took off, bumping over stones and careering round trees. The friends clung tightly onto Polly's present.

Suddenly, Babs noticed a sheep standing in their path.

"GET OUT OF THE WAY!" they all yelled, as the board rushed relentlessly onwards.

But the silly sheep was swept up and carried along with them until an overhanging branch whisked it away again.

The skateboard bumped its way down the hill until it reached the road. Then one of the wheels fell off in a shower of sparks.

"Oh, no!" cried Duke.

They all gripped each other tightly as the board teetered and swerved along the road – heading straight for an oncoming truck.

"*Aaaarrrrggghhh!*" the friends cried.

The skateboard emerged unscathed from under the wheels of the truck, and careered over a crash barrier, sending Duke, Babs and the parcel flying.

Duke and the parcel landed on a snow-covered rooftop.

Babs was flung into a fir tree. She slid gently to the ground in a flurry of snow.

Archie, however, clung by the tips of his paws to the end of the skateboard, which had finally come to a halt over a dizzying drop, wondering what his next move should be.

Just then a curious robin landed on his head.

"Shoo! Clear off!" muttered Archie, crossly.

Unfortunately, the weight of the little robin was too much. Archie just couldn't get a grip. His paws slowly slipped from the board and he fell...

"*Aaaaghhhh!*"

Over in the dark playground where Babs had landed, strange noises were making her nervous.

"Hello?" called Babs. "Anyone there?"

Suddenly, she saw a horrible cat staring down at her from one of the swings.

"Oh c... c... crikey!" Babs fled as fast as her little hamster legs could go.

The cat chased her up the steps of the slide and down the other side.

Babs rolled into the snow at the bottom, finally bumping up against a tree.

Behind her, the cat was tumbling over in the snow, becoming a snowball cat!

Closer and closer it rolled towards Babs... then a large lump of snow dropped right onto it from the branches of a tree above.

"I make that hamsters one, cats nil," said Babs, smugly.

Archie, meanwhile, shook himself clear of a snowdrift and checked he was still in one piece. "I'd better go and find Babs and Duke before they get themselves into some horrible pickle without me. Hang on, you two! Help is at hand!" He strode off confidently… and disappeared into a hole.

Back on the rooftop, a pigeon landed beside Duke.

"All right?" he asked. "Don't get many guinea pigs up on roofs. How d'you get here then?"

"It's a long story," said Duke, glumly.

"I've got all night," said the pigeon.

Duke shrugged. "Well…" He related every mournful detail of his day.

The pigeon's eyes began to droop.

"I'm not boring you am I?" Duke asked.

Among the houses below, Babs leapt in fright as her own shadow loomed up beside her.

She gasped. A shadow meant that the sun was rising: *it was nearly morning!* They didn't have much time left to find Polly.

After struggling out of the hole, Archie wandered into a garden.

"Babs! Duke! It's your old friend, Archie!" he called.

Suddenly, a very fierce, unfriendly bulldog barrelled towards him, growling and barking. Archie stood transfixed.

Fortunately, the dog's lead pulled it up short just inches away.

"Oh, bad luck," said Archie, nipping smartly back through the fence.

Up on the snowy rooftop, Duke sat with his head in his paws.

"I wish I hadn't come!" he moaned.

Two more pigeons flew down.

"What's up with him?" asked one.

"He's having one of those days," replied the first pigeon.

"Maybe we ought to cheer him up," said the new arrivals.

More pigeons came. They entertained Duke with a wonderful concert of jokes, impersonations, songs and dance, and he soon found himself grinning and laughing. So he didn't notice the parcel begin to slide down the roof...

"Uh-oh!" said the pigeons.

"What? Oh, carrots...!" Duke dived after the parcel and grabbed at the ribbon as it sailed down over the guttering.

"*DUKE!*"

It was Babs!

The pigeons caught the parcel and gently carried it to the ground while Duke made his way down the drainpipe.

"We've no time to lose, Duke," said Babs. "It's nearly morning!"

"What's the point?" asked Duke. "We've lost Archie and we still don't know where Polly lives."

"Polly?" said the pigeon. "Freckles and that? I know where she lives."

"You do?" asked Babs.

"'Bout three roofs to the left, past two drainpipes; third chimney to the right and straight ahead as the pigeon flies..."

Babs grinned. "Well, let's go!"

Archie, meanwhile, was hobbling down the street, grumbling about the ice between his toes. "How's a chap supposed to save the day with his feet iced up?"

Then he saw a pair of small wellington boots left on a doorstep. Just what he needed!

Archie tried to put them on.

"Wait a minute, there's some of that writing stuff inside this boot. P-O-L-L-Y! How many Pollys can there be in one village?" he said.

Archie gazed up at the house. "She must live *here!*"

While Archie was figuring out what he was going to say when he knocked on the front door, the pigeons flew Babs, Duke and the parcel across the rooftops.

"Ooooh! Great view from up here, Babs!" grinned Duke.

"Yeah! Hey – this must be Polly's house!" said Babs.

The pigeons carefully set them down onto the snowy roof.

"Now," said Babs, wasting no time. "All we have to do is get the parcel down the chimney!"

“Down the chimney?” said Duke. “Couldn’t we just… erm… leave it on the doorstep?”

“No, Duke,” said Babs. “If a thing’s worth doing, it’s worth doing properly.”

Babs and Duke looked up at the chimney. Then they looked at each other. Neither knew how they were going to get the parcel down it.

“I know!” said Duke, suddenly inspired.

As the morning sun shone golden over the sleeping village, Duke peered into the chimney, anxiously watching his plan being put into action. One by one, the pigeons had grasped each other’s wings and made a feathery chain right down inside the chimney. At the bottom of the chain was the parcel with Babs holding tightly as it swayed and bumped its sooty way down.

At last the parcel stopped with a jolt in the fireplace of Polly's bedroom.

Polly was in bed, fast asleep.

Babs gazed around the room with dizzy pleasure, then she set to work…

A small Christmas tree stood in the corner of the bedroom. Babs quickly tore off some of the red paper round its base to make a cloak for herself. Some wisps of cotton wool made a beard.

"Ho, ho, ho!" she said, quietly.

Then she pushed the parcel over to Polly's bed.

"Happy Christmas, Polly!"

Polly stirred. Her eyes opened and she looked sleepily down at the tiny Santa Claus standing by her bed.

"'appy Chrissmss…" she murmured, before falling asleep again.

Babs blew Polly a kiss, then scampered back to the fireplace.

The pigeon chain pulled her back up the chimney.

Just as Babs stepped out onto the roof, the pigeons suddenly took flight in a feathery panic.

"'Ere, what's going on?" said Duke.

Reeerooowwwww!

"Oh, crikey! Not you again!" said Babs, as she saw the horrible cat creeping towards them across the roof. "RUUUUUNNNN!"

Babs and Duke fled in different directions.

Babs leapt to the roof next door. Duke slid down the roof and ran along the gutter instead. Then, as the cat streaked towards him, Duke launched himself into space…

…slipped down the next roof…

…made a grab for the gutter…

…slid down an icicle…

…and landed on the porch.

Duke looked up. Gulp! The cat grinned down at him and prepared to jump.

Just then, something caught hold of the cat's tail. It was Babs!

The furious cat swung the plucky little hamster towards the Town Hall clock.

Babs hung onto the minute hand while the cat waited for her to fall.

Suddenly, *WHOP!* A snowball hit the cat square in the face.

"Bingo!" cried Archie. "One false move, my furry friend, and you'll be enjoying another snow sandwich!"

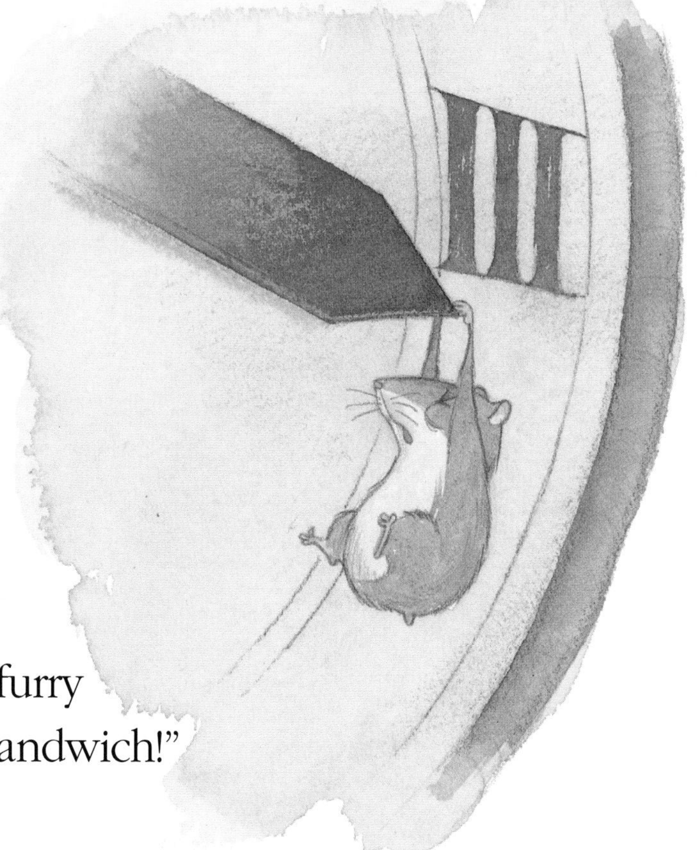

Ignoring his warning, the cat leapt at Archie.

Reeerooowwwww!

"*Aaaagghhh!*" cried the rabbit.

Together, Archie and the cat hurtled over and over, down and down.

Fortunately, two pigeons caught hold of Archie's ears and carried him to safety.

The cat, however, crash-landed in a dustbin full of smelly rubbish and gave up the chase in disgust.

"You guys were heroes," said Duke to Babs and Archie when they were together again.

"You were a hero, too, Duke," said a voice behind them. It was Santa Claus! "You didn't want to be involved, but you came to help your friends. A reluctant hero is the greatest hero of all, you know. Thank you all for delivering Polly's present. The least I can do is give you a lift home!"

Delighted, the three friends piled into Santa's sleigh – where they found the snowman, who had come along for the ride.

“Ho, ho ho!” roared Santa as they streaked away. “I love Christmas!”

Christmas morning dawned, and a little girl called Polly picked up the present by her bed. 'To dear freckle-faced Polly, love Santa' said the label. Polly unwrapped it and took out a beautiful snowstorm. Inside the globe were three little figures: a rabbit, a guinea pig and a hamster. Clearly they were good friends. Polly was delighted. It was her most magical present ever.

THE END